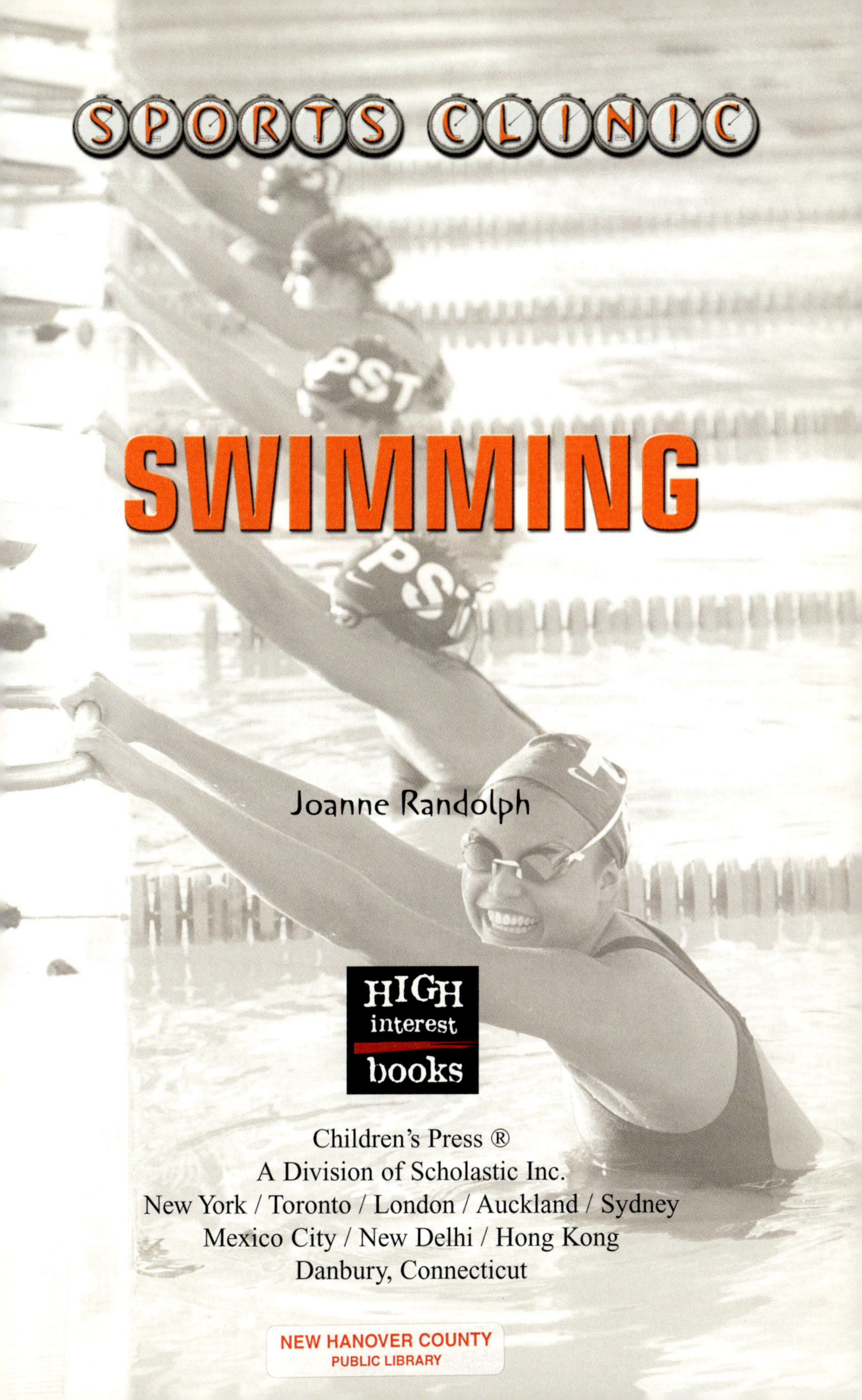

SPORTS CLINIC

SWIMMING

Joanne Randolph

HIGH interest books

Children's Press ®
A Division of Scholastic Inc.
New York / Toronto / London / Auckland / Sydney
Mexico City / New Delhi / Hong Kong
Danbury, Connecticut

For Linda, a great swim instructor and an even better mom

Thanks to The Plantation Swim Team, Plantation, FL

Book Design: Laura Stein
Contributing Editor: Matthew Pitt
Photo Credits: Cover and all other photos by Maura Boruchow; p. 12 © Neal Preston/Corbis; pp. 14–15, 22 by Kim Sonsky; p. 20 © Duomo/Corbis; p. 21 © AFP/Corbis; p. 23 © Bruce Burkhardt/Corbis; p. 25 © TempSport/Corbis; p. 41 © Reuters NewMedia Inc./Corbis

Visit Children's Press on the Internet at:
http://publishing.grolier.com

Library of Congress Cataloging-in-Publication Data

Randolph, Joanne.
Swimming / Joanne Randolph.
p. cm. — (Sports clinic)
Includes bibliographical references and index.
ISBN 0-516-23165-0 (lib. bdg.) — ISBN 0-516-29561-6 (pbk.)
1. Swimming—Juvenile literature. [1. Swimming.] I. Title. II. Series.

GV837.6 .R36 2001
797.2'1—dc21

00-066048

Printed in the United States of America.
1 2 3 4 5 6 7 8 9 10 R 05 04 03 02 01

CONTENTS

INTRODUCTION

When I first joined the swim team, I tried to win races by moving my arms very quickly. All the young swimmers did. The real race seemed to be who could splash the most. We all swam wildly down the pool, kicking and slapping the water. Then I began to watch more experienced swimmers. They swam smoothly and could breathe easily. They'd finish the race while I was still stuck in the water. How did they make it look so easy?

Coaches used to think that swimming lap after lap was the only way to improve. It is important to swim laps and build your endurance. But you won't become a great swimmer without learning to perfect your swimming strokes.

This book helps you master the strokes. It also teaches you other tricks. You'll learn how to explode off the blocks. You'll learn how to make great flip turns. This book teaches you the skills you need to be a winning swimmer.

To become a great swimmer, you must do more than just swim laps. You must learn to perfect your swimming strokes.

ONE

GETTING YOUR FEET WET

Diving into a pool's cool blue water is my favorite thing to do. The splash makes a beautiful sound. The lightness of your body as you float to the top is amazing. No other sport gives you that feeling. Have you ever wondered why you float in water and how your body helps propel you through it? Water is denser, or heavier, than air. In fact, it is 1,000 times more dense! The resistance of water against our bodies can make it hard to swim fast. However, this same resistance allows us to move while underwater. When we swim, we use our arms and legs to pull against the water. The force of our pull moves us forward through the water. But because the water is so dense, it also drags against our bodies.

One key to becoming a better swimmer is to balance resistance and drag. You need to reduce the water's drag. At the same time, you need to increase your use of the water's resistance when you pull through a stroke. How do you do it? Just move faster, right? Wrong! The true key to swimming faster is having better technique. If your technique is correct, it actually should take fewer strokes to finish a race.

It's helpful to watch Olympic swimmers. They barely splash as they swim the length of the pool. Each splash is a sign that the water is slowing them down. Swimming is especially hard when you don't do the strokes correctly. Once you understand how and why each stroke works, you'll be well on your way to becoming a better swimmer.

Let's look at some basics for each stroke. We'll begin with the freestyle, or crawl.

Focusing on balance will make you faster in the freestyle and make the most of your ability to float. Your chest is the part of your body that floats best. If you push your chest into the water, the bottom half of your body rises. If you lift your head, your legs sink. So try to think of your head as part of your chest. Push both your head and chest down until your hips and legs rise. It might feel awkward at first. Once you master this technique, you won't have to fight to float. You won't have to work so hard to kick, either.

When swimming freestyle, keep both your head and chest down.

PULL

Now that you're balanced, it's time to start moving. You're probably used to pulling your arm straight down once it enters the water. To improve your speed, you need to change your pull, or the motion of your arms. Moving each arm in a spiral motion gives you more force to move through the water. It also reduces the amount of drag. As your hand enters the water, stretch it out. Then, with your palm tilted slightly away from your body, move

A good freestyle stroke starts by stretching out your hand as it enters the w
In the follow-through position, your palm should be facing your hip.

your arm to the side as you push down with it. Turn your palm toward your body. Pull your hand down and toward your body. As you lift your arm back out of the water, your palm should be facing your hip with the pinky up.

FUN FACT:

The crawl is often the first stroke learned by U.S. swimmers. In other countries, such as France, Scotland, and Germany, the breaststroke is taught first.

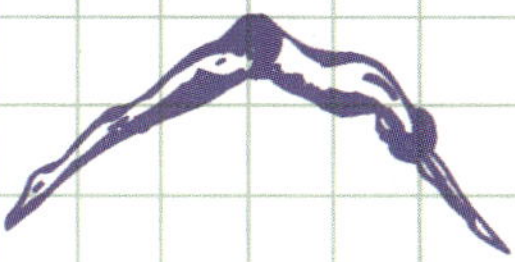

KICK

When swimming freestyle, use the flutter kick. Be careful that you don't kick so hard that your heels come out of the water. The kick won't increase your speed much, but it will help your balance. Use a kickboard to practice. Focus on kicking just hard enough to keep your legs aligned with your body. Do not try to drive yourself down the pool with the force of your kick. The best swimmers barely kick at all.

Using a kickboard, Olympic swimmer Pablo Morales perfects his balancing ability.

Freestyle swimmers use their hips to gain greater swimming force during the pull.

ROLL

If you use your hips well, you'll gain greater swimming force. When your left arm comes out of the water, start rolling your hips so you'll be on your left side, too. Your right hip will point toward the surface. Begin your pull, releasing your hips to spring back to normal. As your right arm comes out of the water, roll onto your right side. Once you get into a rhythm, you will feel how much more power your stroke has.

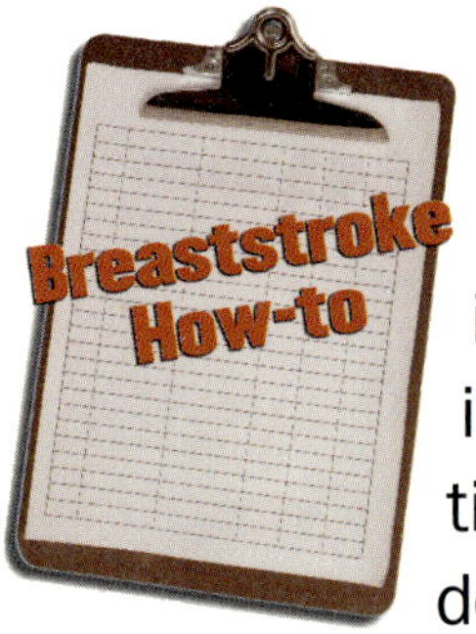

The breaststroke is not the fastest stroke but, in some ways, it's the easiest. It allows you to breathe more easily. It takes advantage of the glide portion of the stroke more than the crawl does. In the breaststroke, the kick is very important. So we'll learn that part first.

KICK

When racing with the breaststroke, two kinds of kicks may be used. The most common is called the whipkick. In this kick, your legs spread apart and come back together in a whipping motion. To

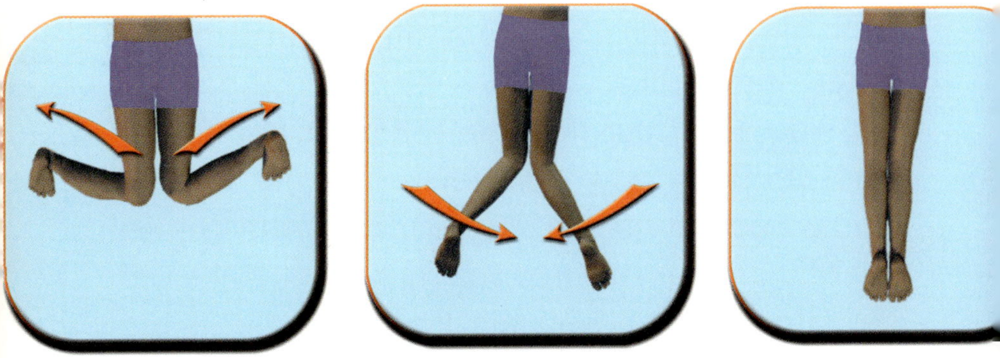

In the whipkick, breaststroke swimmers swivel the bottom parts of their legs in a circular motion. Then they whip their legs back together to repeat the kick.

start the whipkick, bring your knees together. Tuck them forward. Next, start the whipping action. With your knees bent, spread your legs apart. Swivel the bottom parts of your legs in a circular motion. Quickly pull them back together. Draw your knees forward again to repeat the motion.

Other swimmers use the frog kick. In this kind of kick, your heels are close together. Your knees are apart as you tuck them forward. As you spread your legs, separate your heels and unbend your knees. Do this until your legs have straightened out. Bring your heels together and draw the knees forward to start the next kick.

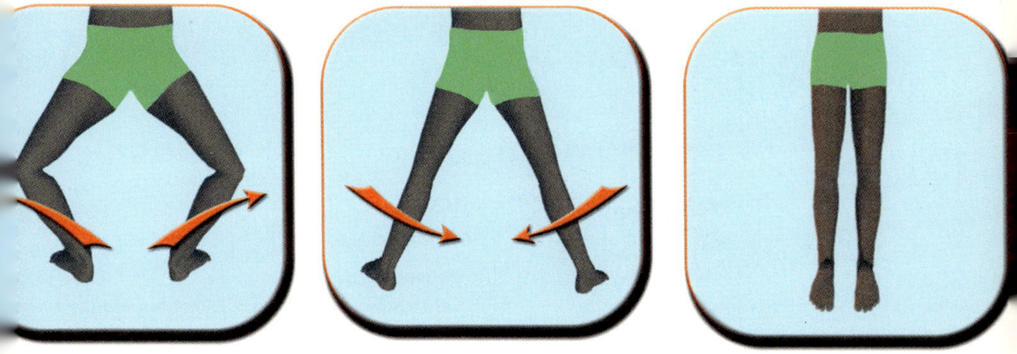

Some of the force of the frog kick comes from separating your heels and tucking your knees forward.

PULL

Begin with your arms stretched out in front of you underwater. Pull your arms apart, just past your shoulder blades. Next, swing your hands together by bending your elbows. Tuck your hands up underneath your chest. While you are doing this, bring your elbows in and breathe.

By starting with their arms fully stretched out in front of them, breaststroke swimmers can make a powerful pull.

FUN FACT:

Breaststroke swimmers used to be disqualified if their heads went underwater. Now they're allowed to submerge their heads. Because of this rule change, many new breaststroke records are being set.

PUTTING IT TOGETHER

To combine the kick and pull, start your stroke in a prone float. This means that you lie on your stomach. Place your arms in front, then pull them out to the sides. Your legs and hips will begin to drop. When you're ready to drive your arms forward, start kicking. Kicking brings your legs up and propels you forward, allowing you to glide easily down the pool. Kicking at this time also lets you lift your head to breathe.

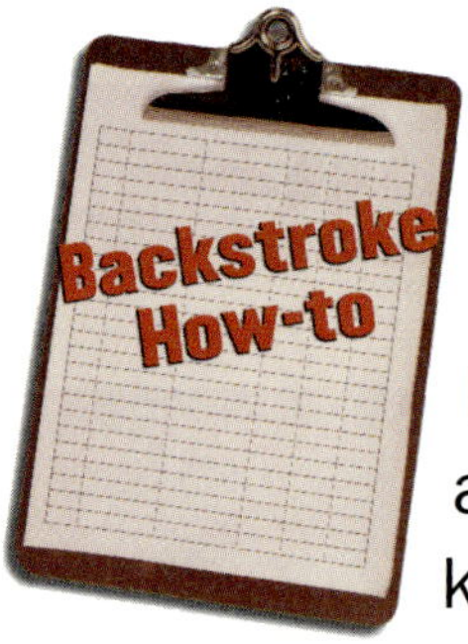

The backstroke is the only racing stroke performed while on your back. It isn't easy for everyone to master. That's partly because it's difficult to see where you are going. However, there are ways to know where you are in the pool. This is called orienting yourself.

Concentrating on an object at the end of the pool will orient you. It also helps you stay in the center of your lane. Focus your eyes on something like the lane flags. When you see flags at the other end of the pool, you'll be about 30 feet from the wall. Count how many strokes it takes to get from the flags to the wall. Once you know that, you'll be able to turn without having to look.

PULL

Your arm will be straight as it leaves the water and bent during the pull. Start by pointing your pinky toward the ceiling. As each arm goes above your head, your shoulder should touch your ear. Drive your arm into the water, bending your elbow. Push your hand below your thigh. Then pull it back to your hip with your palm facing your body. Just before you lift your arm out, twist your wrist. When your arm slices out of the water, the pinky again will be pointing toward the ceiling, ready to start the next stroke.

It's also important to roll as you pull. You should roll to the side you are pulling from. In other words, as you pull with your right

This swimmer's pinky is pointed toward the ceiling. She is ready to begin the pull of her next backstroke.

arm, roll your body to the right. Your left shoulder will rise out of the water.

Backstroke swimmers rely on the flutter kick to maintain their balance during a race.

KICK

Freestyle and backstroke swimmers use the same kick: the flutter kick. To keep their legs from sinking, most swimmers have to kick more in the backstroke than in the crawl. You can use the same balance technique in the backstroke to keep your legs up. Just think about pressing your chest into the water as you swim.

For most swimmers, the butterfly is the hardest stroke. There are two keys to perfecting it. One is power and the other is technique. If you're strong in the shoulders and back, this stroke will be easier. You still can be a great butterflier even if you aren't the strongest kid on the block. If you learn the proper steps, you'll be faster and better than swimmers who are strong but do the stroke poorly.

Great technique, not great strength, is the main key to swimming success.

KICK

The dolphin kick is used in the butterfly. This is a double-leg kick. You keep your legs together the whole time. It looks as if you're kicking with a tail, not with two feet, which is why it's called a dolphin kick. The kick should start with your legs out straight. As you drop your hips, bend both knees. Then, drive your legs down to straighten them. Lift your hips. Finally, move your legs back in line with your body. All these motions must be completed

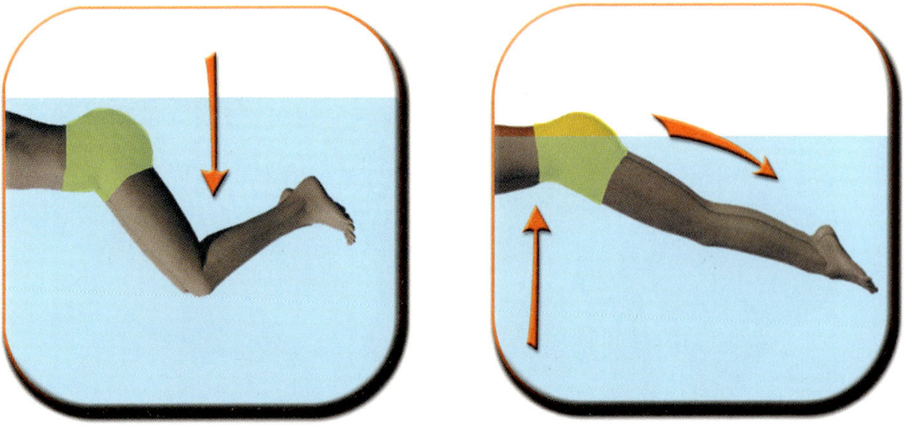

Swimmers who use the dolphin kick look as though they're kicking with a tail, and not their feet.

very quickly. In the butterfly, two dolphin kicks are completed for each single arm stroke.

PULL

Just as with the breaststroke, you pull with both arms at once. The difference is that the butterfly is done overhand. Your arms enter the water in front of you, hands just outside the shoulders.

When you finish the pull portion of the butterfly stroke, your pinkies should be pointing upward.

Bend your elbows slightly and turn your palms slightly outward. Once your arms are in the water, straighten them and begin to move them downward. As you pull, your arms will move in a keyhole pattern. You'll start by sweeping your arms outward with the palms facing out. Once your arms are outstretched, start to pull inward and down. Finally, pull your hands up toward your body and in toward your hips. Turn your hands so that the pinkies point upward at the moment you leave the water. As your hands finish the pull, your elbows exit the water first.

PUTTING IT TOGETHER

Timing the kick with the pull is very important. This is called synchronization. Your body should move through the water in an "S" movement. The first kick starts as your arms begin their pull. As your arms pass beneath your shoulders, turn your head to the side and take a well-earned breath. The second kick comes halfway through the pull.

This kick helps drive your shoulders and head out of the water.

Beginning butterfly swimmers usually dive too deeply before the pull. If you dive too deeply, it's hard to kick your legs properly. It then becomes difficult to get your upper body and arms out of the water for the next stroke. A deep dive throws your timing off and slows you down.

Expert butterfly swimmers like Olympian Summer Sanders know how important it is to time the kick with the pull.

TWO

OFF THE BLOCKS

In many races, swimmers are evenly matched. Valuable seconds can be gained by a great start. How fast you get off the blocks can mean the difference between winning and losing.

There are three components, or parts, to a good start. The first component is the ability to react to the gun quickly. Another is how fast and far you push through the water after you dive. The last is how streamlined you can swim underwater before coming up for air. When your body is streamlined, it's in the best shape to reduce drag.

To get off to a good start in a race, you must be able to react quickly to the starting gun.

Starts

There are two types of starts. Choose whichever is most comfortable. The first is known as a track start. With this start, you look as if you're about to run a race, not swim one. Stand with one foot at the front edge of the block. Your other leg is behind you. Once your feet are in place, bend at the waist and grab the front edge of the block. When the gun is fired, drive off the block. Throw your arms out until the moment before you hit the water.

The hands should enter first, then the head, and then the body. Make sure your dive is shallow. If it's too deep, you'll waste time getting back to the surface. Once you're in the water, glide with your arms over your head for two seconds before starting to kick. Try to reach the surface before you lose the speed from your start. If you're doing the breaststroke, make sure your head breaks the surface before you're halfway through the second stroke. Practice your entry until you can make it halfway down the length of the pool before you start swimming.

A swimmer's body should be fully stretched out when it enters the water.

The other kind of block start is called a grab start. This is the more traditional start. Stand with your feet together, bent at the waist. Again, your toes and fingers should be right at the block's edge. When the starting gun is fired, you should leave the block in the same way as the track start.

Starting Backward

You use the blocks differently when you race backstroke. You're already in the water when the starting gun fires. Before it does, grab the rung on the front of the blocks. Tuck your knees to your chest, placing your toes close to the water's surface.

When you're getting set, use the rung to lift yourself out of the water as much as possible. Get ready for the gun to fire. Once it does, you need to launch yourself backward with as much force as possible. Throw your arms back over your head and be sure to enter the water hands first. Once underwater, keep your hands above your head and glide for two seconds. Then start kicking, using the flutter kick. Make your first stroke underwater and then pop to the surface.

The key to a backstroke start is launching from the blocks with a powerful force.

4 FT.

THREE

THE TURNS

Halfway through the race, you'll encounter a big obstacle—the wall at the end of the pool. At this point, you must make one of two turns. The turn you use depends on the kind of stroke you're doing.

Two-Hand Touch Turn

This turn is used in the breaststroke and butterfly. As you approach the wall, touch it with both hands. Bring your knees under the touch, placing your feet on the wall. Pull one arm away from the wall and turn to the side, rolling your shoulder. Thrust your head underwater, throwing your other arm overhead and into the pool. Push off with both arms overhead and hold the position for three counts. Pull your arms down to your sides and

The two-hand touch turn is used in the breaststroke and butterfly.

hold for two seconds. Then bring your hands to your chest while kicking out. Push your arms straight out and glide.

After turning in the butterfly stroke, you should do four or five dolphin kicks before resuming your swim. You'll travel underwater very quickly this way.

Flip Turns

With a two-hand touch turn, you must stop moving for a few seconds as you get set to push. In a close race, these are seconds you cannot afford to lose. Flip turns shave valuable seconds off your freestyle or backstroke racing times.

Start your flip, or somersault, when you are two strokes away from the wall. Instead of pulling

With flip turns, swimmers use somersaults to lower their racing times.

through that stroke, drop your shoulders. Drive your head toward your knees and do a fast somersault. Your feet should land against the wall with your knees bent. While still on your back, push off from the wall. Your arms will be above your head, hands overlapping. This puts you in a streamlined position. Begin to roll onto your stomach as you kick, keeping your arms above your head. Once on your stomach, keep kicking. At the count of four, pull your lead arm down and resume your normal stroke.

The most important key to a good backstroke flip turn is knowing how many strokes you take to reach the wall. Start your turn when you're two strokes away. Take one backstroke pull, then roll to your stomach as you do one freestyle pull into your flip. You'll complete the turn as instructed above, except for one difference: you won't roll onto your stomach after pushing off from the wall.

FOUR

PUTTING IT ALL TOGETHER

Hard work is the best recipe for swimming success. While you don't have to swim miles of laps, you should devote enough time in the pool to perfecting your technique. Focus on doing the strokes properly. Learn to glide more and move farther with each stroke. Swimming laps builds strength, endurance, and confidence.

Don't forget to develop your starts and turns, too. This actually can be a nice break from swimming laps. The more you repeat starts and turns in practice, the more natural it will feel during races.

In addition to swimming laps, make sure you work hard developing your starts and turns.

Another thing to practice is picturing how the stroke, dive, or turn is supposed to look. This is called visualization. Watch champion swimmers closely, and ask your coach if you can view videotaped swim meets. The more you see what your body should be doing, the easier it will be to imitate it. Visualization is like swimming laps in your mind. While in the pool, pay attention to how each stroke, turn, or dive feels when you've done it correctly. Your brain will start to warn you when you're doing something wrong. When it does, take a moment to change your technique until it feels right again.

Eating a balanced diet is especially important when you're training. Your body and brain need fuel and the right vitamins to perform at their peak. If you don't eat properly, you'll feel sluggish, and your times won't reflect your hard efforts. As a swimmer, you rely heavily on your body to perform well. Make sure that your diet gives you the tools you need.

The Food Guide Pyramid

A Guide to Daily Food Choices

FUN FACT:

Swimmers' bodies need lots of protein (meats, fish, beans, and poultry) and carbohydrates (breads and grains) for energy. Fruits and vegetables replenish vitamins that help your muscles heal and grow stronger. Also, be sure to get enough calcium so your bones stay strong.

As much fun as swimming is, it can wear down your body. Make sure you sleep for at least eight hours each night. Getting a full night's rest is the best way to recharge tired muscles. Also, getting enough sleep will help you feel ready to tackle schoolwork and swim practices like the champion that you are!

It may seem that Olympic athletes were born to win. In fact, it takes years of hard work to become a champion.

USA
USA
USA

NEW WORDS

components parts of something

dense very heavy or thick

dolphin kick a kick in which the swimmer's legs are together

efficient without wasting energy

endurance the ability to do something for a long time without stopping

flutter kick a kick in which both legs whip back and forth

frog kick a kick that begins with the heels together

mastered having perfected a skill

orienting knowing where you are while in the pool

NEW WORDS

propel to drive an object forward

resistance a force that slows motion

streamlined shaped to reduce resistance

synchronization kicking and pulling at the same time

technique proper form

whipkick a kick where the legs whip apart to produce energy

For Further Reading

Anderson, Dave
The Story of the Olympics
New York: HarperCollins Juvenile Books, 2000.

Guzman, Ruben J.
Swimming Drills for Every Stroke
Australia: Human Kinetics Publishers, 1998.

Page, Jason
Swimming: Sprints, Medleys, Diving, Water Polo, & Lots, Lots More
Minneapolis: Lerner Publishing Group, 2000.

Rouse, Jeff
The Young Swimmer
New York: Dorling Kindersley Publishing, 1997.

RESOURCES

Organizations

YMCA of the USA
101 North Wacker Drive
Chicago, IL 60606
(312) 977-0031

YWCA of the USA
Empire State Building
350 Fifth Avenue, Suite 301
New York, NY 10118

RESOURCES

Web Sites

USA Swimming Official Web Site

http://www.usa-swimming.org/swimkids/

This Web site includes biographies, photos, Olympic memories, and quotes of record-breaking swimmers to inspire swimmers everywhere.

Swimming

http://swimming.about.com/recreation/swimming/msub_famous_swimmers.htm

This Web site features how-to articles, the latest news, and links to the Web sites of swimming legends.

INDEX

About the Author

Joanne Randolph is a freelance writer and editor of children's educational books. She has been swimming since she was four years old.